Note to parents, carers and teachers

Read it yourself is a series of modern stories, favourite characters and traditional tales written in a simple way for children who are learning to read. The books can be read independently or as part of a guided reading session.

Each book is carefully structured to include many high-frequency words vital for first reading. The sentences on each page are supported closely by pictures to help with understanding, and to offer lively details to talk about.

The books are graded into four levels that progressively introduce wider vocabulary and longer stories as a reader's ability and confidence grows.

Ideas for use

- Begin by looking through the book and talking about the pictures. Has your child heard this story before?

- Help your child with any words he does not know, either by helping him to sound them out or supplying them yourself.

- Developing readers can be concentrating so hard on the words that they sometimes don't fully grasp the meaning of what they're reading. Answering the puzzle questions at the end of the book will help with understanding.

For more information and advice on Read it yourself and book banding, visit www.ladybird.com/readityourself

Book
Band
5

Level 1 is ideal for children who have received some initial reading instruction. Each story is told very simply, using a small number of frequently repeated words.

Special features:

Opening pages introduce key story words

Large, clear type

"Can we play a computer game with you?" says Peppa.

"Yes, you can play your game," says Daddy Pig.

Careful match between story and pictures

Educational Consultant: Geraldine Taylor
Book Banding Consultant: Kate Ruttle

LADYBIRD BOOKS

UK | USA | Canada | Ireland | Australia
India | New Zealand | South Africa

Ladybird Books is part of the Penguin Random House group of companies
whose addresses can be found at global.penguinrandomhouse.com.

www.penguin.co.uk   www.puffin.co.uk   www.ladybird.co.uk

Penguin
Random House
UK

Text adapted from Peppa Pig's Family Computer, first published by Ladybird Books, 2012
This edition first published by Ladybird Books, 2016
005

Text and illustrations copyright © Astley Baker Davies Ltd/Entertainment One UK Ltd, 2016
Adapted by Ellen Philpott
The moral right of the author has been asserted

This book is based on the
TV Series 'Peppa Pig'
'Peppa Pig' is created by
Neville Astley and Mark Baker
Peppa Pig © Astley Baker Davies Ltd/
Entertainment One UK Ltd, 2003

www.peppapig.com

Printed in China

A CIP catalogue record for this book is
available from the British Library

ISBN: 978-0-24121-813-6

MIX
Paper from
responsible sources
FSC® C018179

The Family Computer

Adaptation written by Ellen Philpott
Based on the TV series *Peppa Pig*. *Peppa Pig* is
created by Neville Astley and Mark Baker

 Peppa

 George

 Daddy Pig

computer

computer game

work

Mummy Pig

7

Mummy Pig has work to do.
She is on the computer.

8

"Daddy," says Peppa.
"Can we go and
see Mummy?"

"Yes, if you can be good,"
says Daddy.

10

11

"Can George and I see you work?" says Peppa.

"Yes, if you can be good," says Mummy.

"Can we play a computer game?" says Peppa.

"No, Peppa, I have work to do," says Mummy.

Mummy Pig has work to do.

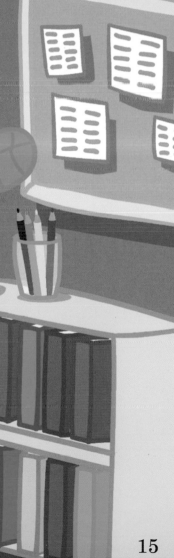

"Can we do your work with you?" says Peppa.

Then she taps the computer.

"No, Peppa!" says Mummy.

17

The computer is not working!

"Sorry, Mummy," says Peppa.

19

"Daddy Pig!" says Mummy. "You are the expert. Can you come and mend the computer?"

"Sorry, I am not very good at mending computers," says Daddy Pig.

Daddy Pig taps
the computer.

He turns it off. Then he
turns it on . . .

Off! On!

"You have mended it, Daddy!" says Peppa.

"Yes, I am an expert at mending computers," says Daddy.

"Can we play a computer game with you?" says Peppa.

"Yes, you can play your game," says Daddy Pig.

27

Peppa and George are playing the computer game. It is a very good game.

"I see the computer is working again!" says Mummy Pig.

How much do you remember about the story of Peppa Pig: The Family Computer? Answer these questions and find out!

- **What is Mummy doing on the computer?**

- **What do Peppa and George ask to do?**

- **How does Daddy Pig mend the computer?**

Look at the pictures from the story and say the order they should go in.

A

B

C

D

Tick the books you've read!

Level 1

Level 2